Stuff!

Reduce, Reuse, Recycle

by
Steven Kroll

illustrated by
Steve Cox

Marshall Cavendish Children

Text copyright © 2009 by Steven Kroll
Illustrations copyright © 2009 by Steve Cox
All rights reserved

Marshall Cavendish Corporation, 99 White Plains Road, Tarrytown, NY 10591
www.marshallcavendish.us/kids

Library of Congress Cataloging-in-Publication Data
Kroll, Steven.
Stuff! : reduce, reuse, recycle / by Steven Kroll ; illustrated by Steve Cox. — 1st ed.
    p. cm.
Summary: Pinch is a pack rat who does not want to give up the possessions that are cluttering his house,
but when he finally is persuaded to sell them at a neighborhood tag sale, he discovers the beauty of
recycling. Includes tips on "reducing, reusing, and recycling."
ISBN 978-0-7614-5570-7
[1. Junk—Fiction. 2. Recycling (Waste)—Fiction. 3. Neighborhood--Fiction. 4. Garage sales—Fiction.
5. Wood rats—Fiction. 6. Rats—Fiction. 7. Animals--Fiction.] I. Cox, Steve, 1961- ill. II. Title.
PZ7.K9225St 2009
[E]--dc22
    2008012915

The art was rendered in mixed media/digital.
Book design by Virginia Pope.
Editor: Margery Cuyler
Printed in China
First edition
1 3 5 6 4 2

This book is printed on recycled paper.

mc **Marshall Cavendish**
Children

For Kathleen
—S.K.

For Edie . . . and all her stuff
—S.C.

Pinch

was a pack rat. He kept everything. He kept piles of magazines and old clothes. He kept toy cars and boats and tools and games and books and puzzles.

There was so much stuff in Pinch's house, it was spilling out onto the street.

One spring day, the other animals in the neighborhood decided to clean up the town and have a tag sale. Bumper Bunny and Heddy Hedgehog marched up to Pinch's door.

Heddy knocked. No answer. She knocked again.
Still no answer.

"Pinch!" she shouted. "Your stuff is making a mess!
Could you donate some of it to our tag sale?"

A groan came from inside the house.

"Noooooooo," wailed Pinch. "I like all my stuff! I don't want to donate any of it!"

"But Pinch," said Bumper, "you've run out of room. If you sell your stuff at our tag sale, people can reuse it."

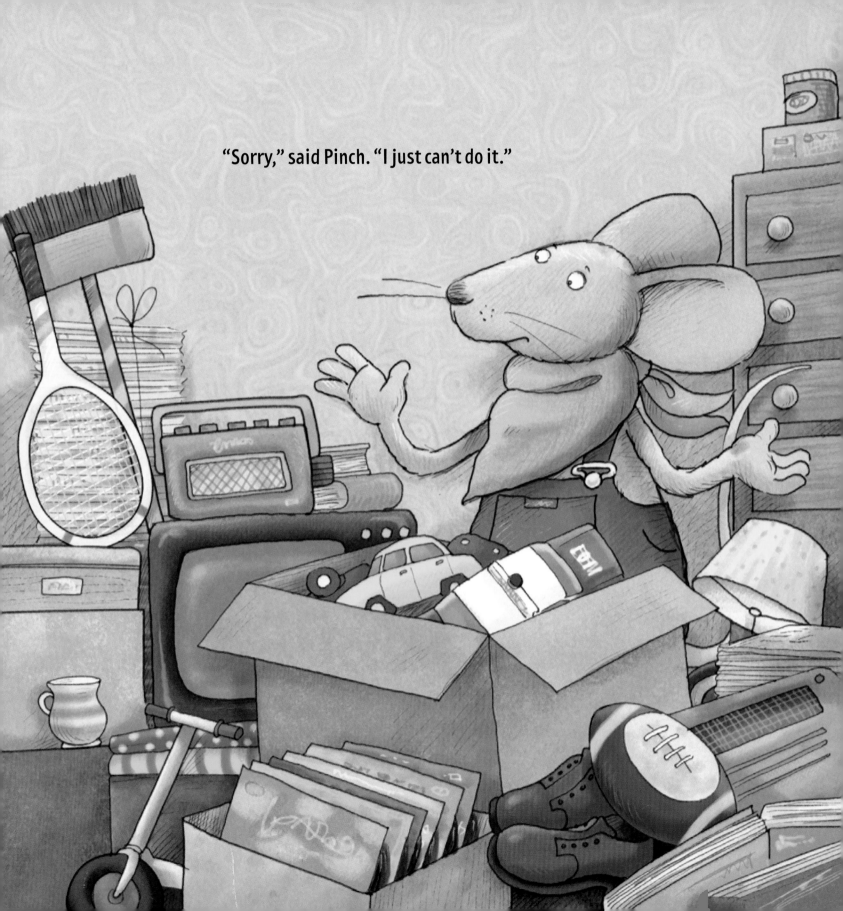

"Sorry," said Pinch. "I just can't do it."

Bumper and Heddy shook their heads and went to join their friends. They picked up trash and gathered newspapers, cans, and bottles for recycling. Then they went to the town square for the tag sale.

From his doorstep, Pinch watched as friends from all over the neighborhood bought clothes and skates and footballs, games and toys and frilly dolls.

"Hey," he said to himself, "maybe I *should* sell some of my stuff. Then I'd make enough money to buy more stuff!"

Pinch got out his old wheelbarrow and loaded it up.
He struggled over to the town square.
"Look who's here," said Heddy Hedgehog.
"Welcome, Pinch. You can use the table by the fence."

Pinch emptied his wheelbarrow.

He went back for another load . . .

and another.

Then he began to sell.
"I hope I make lots of money," he said.
Old shirts went. Tools went.
Toy cars and boats and puzzles went.

"Oh, wow!" said a little girl chipmunk.
"Look at this beautiful doll! I've wanted a doll like this for a long time."
"I never imagined that doll was beautiful," thought Pinch. "It just lay at the back of my closet."

"That red truck's awesome," said a little boy bunny.
"I hope it doesn't cost too much."

"Not for you," Pinch said.
He sold the truck and watched
the boy push it along in the grass.
"I guess that truck *is* awesome," he said.
"I just never noticed."

By the end of the day, Pinch had sold everything he'd
brought and was smiling at all the animals enjoying his stuff.
Next to him, Heddy Hedgehog was counting her money.

"Let's use the money we made to buy a tree," Heddy said.
Pinch cleared his throat. "*All* of it?" he asked.
"Well, sure, Pinch," said Bumper Bunny. "That's the point.
We want to make our town pretty as well as clean."
"Hmmm," said Pinch. "Let me think about it."

Pinch went home to his very clean house.

He ate dinner in his very clean kitchen.

He went to bed in his very clean bedroom. And he thought about how nice it was *not* to live with stuff everywhere.

Then he thought about how his friends wanted to spend all the money from the tag sale on a tree, and he got an idea.

The next afternoon, Pinch marched into the town square. Behind him stretched a long line of wheelbarrows.

"What's going on?" asked Heddy and Bumper.
Pinch grinned. "All my relatives have brought
their stuff," he said.

Everyone watched as the pack rats emptied their wheelbarrows into a huge pile.

"Tomorrow we're going to have another tag sale," Pinch declared, "and we'll make enough money to buy a dozen trees!"

"HOORAY FOR PINCH!"

WITHDRAWN

Washington County Free Library
100 South Potomac Street
Hagerstown, MD 21740-5504
www.washcolibrary.org

3 2395 00854 8865